To Julia and Carolyn

Henry Holt and Company, LLC

Publishers since 1866

115 West 18th Street, New York, New York 10011

Henry Holt is a registered trademark of Henry Holt and Company, LLC

Copyright © 2005 by Dan Yaccarino

All rights reserved.

Distributed in Canada by H. B. Fenn & Company Ltd.

ISBN-10: 0-8050-7493-7

Hand lettering by David Gatti

Printed in Mexico

The artist used gouache on watercolor paper to create
the illustrations for this book.

THE BIRTHDAY FISH

DAN YACCARINO

Henry Holt and Company • New York

Cynthia loved ponies.

All she could think about was ponies.

Every birthday Cynthia wished for a pony,
and every birthday she got something else.

This year, when Cynthia blew out the candles and made her wish, she just knew things would be different. She would get a pony, and she would name him Marigold.

After eating some cake, Cynthia ran to open her
presents. When she saw the gift from her parents,
she thought it must be a very small pony.

But it wasn't. It was a goldfish.

Cynthia was so upset that she took the goldfish and started to pour it down the drain.

"Oh, please don't do that!" a little voice said.

Cynthia looked around but saw no one.

"Oh, please don't dump me down the drain!" the little voice spoke again.

It was the goldfish.

Cynthia told him she wanted a pony, not a goldfish. *Every* year she wished for a pony when she blew out the candles on her birthday cake.

Every year she put a pony on her Christmas list. But no matter how good she was, she never got a pony.

"I am a magical fish," said the little fish, "and I will give you what you wish for if you will take me to a lake and set me free."

Cynthia wished for two ponies, put the fishbowl in her toy stroller, and set off.

The stroller hit a bump in the road that made
the goldfish splash about in his bowl.
"Slow down please!" shouted the goldfish.

After that, Cynthia slowed down
and watched carefully for bumps.

They passed a cat, who eyed the goldfish hungrily.
"Oh, my," said the goldfish, "I don't like the way
that cat is looking at me." Cynthia crossed the street.

They passed some boys playing ball. "Be careful!" Cynthia shouted.

"Thank you," said the goldfish.

They came to a pet store. "Would you like
something to eat?" Cynthia asked.
"If you would be so kind," said the goldfish.
So she bought some fish food.

They walked under the hot sun. Cynthia placed
her poncho over the bowl to shade the fish.

At last, they arrived at the lake. They sat
and watched the sunset together.
"It's late," said the goldfish.

"Yes, it is," replied Cynthia.
"Let's go home now, Marigold."